Hello Kitty Hello Love!

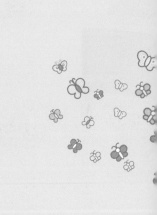

Hello Kitty

Hello Love!

Harry N. Abrams, Inc., Publishers

Hello Kitty loves to give presents to her friends. Today she is planning to give a present to Daniel, her very special friend.

What will Daniel love as a present? Hello Kitty telephones each of her other friends for ideas!

Hello Kitty loves rainbows, and her friend Joey loves rainbows too!

But how will Hello Kitty
ever be able to wrap
a rainbow?

Hello Kitty loves butterflies,
and her friend Fifi loves
butterflies too!

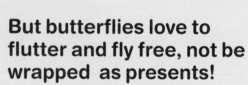

But butterflies love to
flutter and fly free, not be
wrapped as presents!

Hello Kitty loves warm breezes, and her friend Kathy loves warm breezes too!

But how will Hello Kitty squeeze a breeze into a box?

Hello Kitty loves to hear birds singing, and her friends Timmy and Tammy love to hear birds singing too!

But Hello Kitty's favorite birds sing best in the trees, not trapped inside boxes!

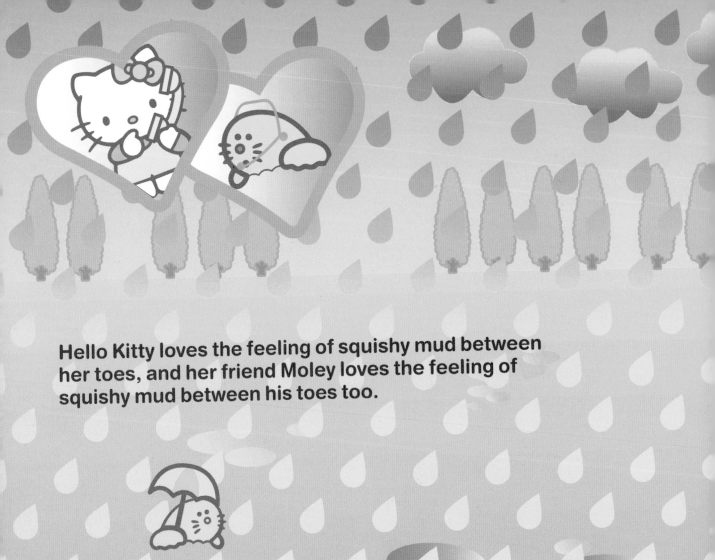

Hello Kitty loves the feeling of squishy mud between her toes, and her friend Moley loves the feeling of squishy mud between his toes too.

But Daniel's mother would not love all that mud in her house, and besides, who would want a box full of mud!

Hello Kitty
wants to
make
Daniel
happy.
What will
she do?

There are so many, many things she and her friends love, but what will Daniel love?

Suddenly Hello Kitty has an idea *she* loves!

And she hopes that
Daniel will love it too!

Hello Kitty is making a present that is like a rainbow. It is full of singing birds and fluttering butterflies.

It is a place where warm breezes blow and where there is always plenty of mud for squishing between toes. Can you guess what it is?

Why, her present is a garden!
And of course Daniel loves it!

Illustration and Design: Roger La Borde and Rob Biddulph
Production Director: Hope Koturo

Library of Congress Cataloging-in-Publication Data

La Borde, Roger.
Hello Kitty, Hello Love! / by Roger La Borde.
p. cm.
Summary: Hello Kitty tries to think of just the right gift for her special friend, one that includes all the things she and her friends like.
ISBN 0-8109-8538-1
[1. Gifts—Fiction. 2. Friendship—Fiction. 3. Cats—Fiction.] I. Title.

PZ7.L1155 He 2003
[E]—dc21
2002014070

Published in 2003 by Harry N. Abrams, Incorporated, New York

Printed and bound in China
10 9 8 7 6 5 4 3 2 1

 Harry N. Abrams, Inc.
100 Fifth Avenue
New York, N.Y. 10011
www.abramsbooks.com

Abrams is a subsidiary of
 LA MARTINIÈRE
GROUPE

Hello Friend !

to :

_____

_____

_____

_____

Hello Friend !

to :

_____

_____

_____

_____

Hello  Kitty

Hello Friend !

to :

_____

_____

_____

_____

Hello  Kitty

Hello Friend !

to :

_____

_____

_____

_____